A Goodnight
Kind of Feeling

Tony Bradman & Clive Scruton

Holiday House/New York

I like that...

getting ready,

come on teddy,

we're on our way out

kind of feeling.

I like that...

bumpety-bump,

big holes to jump,

rolling and tumbling along

kind of feeling.

I like that...
lovely fresh air, trees and grass everywhere
kind of feeling.

I like that...

scary quack-quack-quack,

I want my fingers back

kind of feeling.

I like that...

whee! down the slide,

can I go for a ride?

kind of feeling.

I like that round and round, up and down,

high above the ground kind of feeling!

I like that...

yummy, yummy, in my tummy,

lunch-time, munch-time, crunch-time

kind of feeling.

I like that...

stroll in the sun,

it's been lots of fun, let's stop at the shops

kind of feeling.

I like that big girls and boys, hundreds of toys,

something for *me* kind of feeling.

I like that...

bumpety-bump,

big holes to jump,

rolling and tumbling home

kind of feeling.

I like that...

end of the day, not much to say,

tickle and laugh,

time for a bath

kind of feeling.

But best of all...

I love that warm and snuggly,

deep and duggly, sleep tight,

don't let the bed bugs bite...

goodnight kind of feeling!